Jim Henson's™ DOOZERS™

Make a Rainbow

adapted by Natalie Shaw
based on the screenplay "The Rainbow Connection"
written by Amanda Smith

Ready-to-Read

Simon Spotlight
New York   London   Toronto   Sydney   New Delhi

SIMON SPOTLIGHT

An imprint of Simon & Schuster Children's Publishing Division

1230 Avenue of the Americas, New York, New York 10020

This Simon Spotlight edition September 2019

© 2019 The Jim Henson Company. JIM HENSON'S mark & logo, DOOZERS mark & logo, characters and elements are trademarks of The Jim Henson Company. All Rights Reserved.

All rights reserved, including the right of reproduction in whole or in part in any form.

SIMON SPOTLIGHT, READY-TO-READ, and colophon are registered trademarks of Simon & Schuster, Inc.

For information about special discounts for bulk purchases, please contact Simon & Schuster Special Sales at 1-866-506-1949 or business@simonandschuster.com.

Manufactured in the United States of America 0719 LAK

10 9 8 7 6 5 4 3 2 1

ISBN 978-1-5344-4548-2 (pb)

ISBN 978-1-5344-4549-9 (hc)

ISBN 978-1-5344-4550-5 (eBook)

Spike, Molly Bolt, and Flex
are at the barn.

"The rain stopped,"
Spike says.

"Look, a rainbow!"

says Flex.

"Daisy Wheel has to

see this!"

Spike says.

"She loves rainbows!"

Spike calls Daisy Wheel

on her watch.

"I do not see a rainbow!"

she says.

"It is by the barn!"

Spike says.

Daisy Wheel comes to

the barn.

The rainbow is gone!

Flex, Molly Bolt, and Spike want to make a rainbow for Daisy Wheel.

First they ask an artist to paint a rainbow!

It is colorful, but it is not a real rainbow.

Next they set up lights.

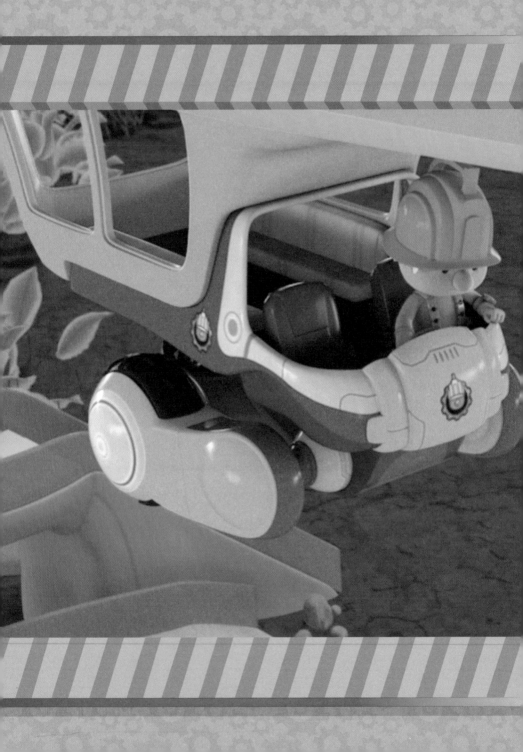

Colors fill the sky.

"All of those colors are
mixed together,"
says Daisy Wheel.

Professor Gimbal wants to help.

He shows the Pod Squad

a special piece of glass.

"What is that?"

Spike asks.

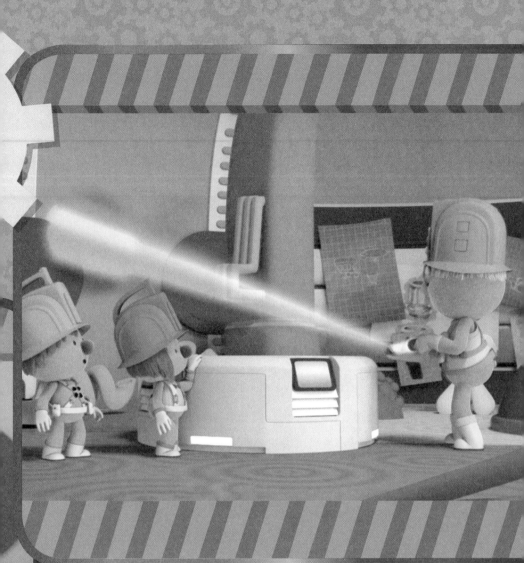

Professor Gimbal says,

"You use it to bend light!"

"The light we see every day is called white light, but it is made of many colors," Professor Gimbal says.

"When white light hits this special glass, the light bends. You can see the colors," he adds.

"It is just like a rainbow!"

says Molly Bolt.

The professor explains,
"The rain bends light just
like this piece of glass."

The Pod Squad can make a real rainbow!

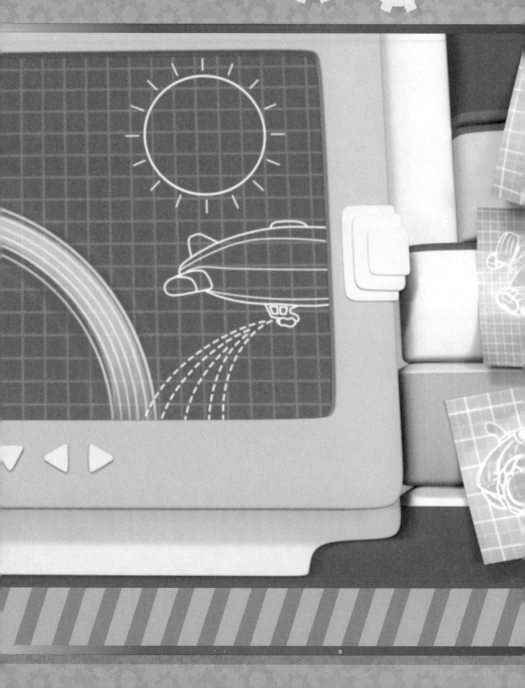

Flex, Spike, and Molly Bolt

spray water in the air.

Then light from the sun

shines through the water.

"It is a real rainbow!"

Daisy Wheel says.

Everyone in Doozer Creek

can see it!

There is nothing to it

when you do, do, do it!